Printed in the United States
By Bookmasters

Candace Says... "You're Not The Boss Of Me."

Lynda C. Wade

Illustrations by Cleoward Sy

Print information available on the last page.

To order additional copies of this book, contact:
Xlibris
1-888-795-4274
www.Xlibris.com
Orders@Xlibris.com

For Candace, my beautiful and beloved daughter. Thank you for your unconditional love.

Thank you mom, for your love, support and encouragement.

Special thanks to The Romney and Davis Family.

"Oh, oh! Mom is up early again." She says, "Candace it's time to get up. Brush your teeth, wash your face and come and eat your breakfast."

I groan as I roll out of bed and whisper, "You're not the boss of me!"

I get out of bed, brush my teeth, wash my face and go have my breakfast.
Mommy gives me my favorite things. Pancakes, turkey bacon and a glass of Milk....hmmm hmmm yummy.

I finish my breakfast while mommy cleans up
the kitchen. I say, "Hey mommy." "What are we
doing today?" "Can you play with me?" "Please?"
Mommy grumbles under her breath.
Today is not a play day for me.
I sigh, "Oh mom you never, ever,
ever play with me."

Then mommy sighs, and smiles. "Candace be a good girl, take a bath and clean your room, we have to go out in a little bit", says mom.
I say, "Okay mommy" and then whisper, "You're not the boss of me!"

Mommy rocks! After I have taken my bath and cleaned my room mommy takes me to the park. Bestest mommy, ever!

At the park I meet Jake and John, twin brothers and twice the terror.

We take turns on the slide and swings, but then things get crazy when I wanted to play princess and Jake and John wanted to play aliens.

Jake and John say, "You have to play what we want to play. Princess games are for babies!" And do you know what I said to them, "You're not the boss of me!"

Mommy and I play a game of soccer and then I ride my bike around the park while mommy strolls behind.

Mommy says, "Candace be careful!" "Candace don't ride too fast!" "Candace watch where you are going and use both hands!"

"OK, mommy!" I yell. And then I whisper, "You're not the boss of me!"

The ice cream truck stops by so mommy and I bought ice cream. My favorite flavor ice cream is cherry and mommy just loves pineapple.
We sit on the park bench enjoying the afternoon together. I love mommy.

After our outing at the park, mommy and I
return home. It has been a long, but fun day.
Mommy sends me up to my room
to get ready for bed.
After I take my bath and brush my teeth I
am ready and all tucked in bed, it's time for a
bedtime story. Mommy reads the one about the
Princess and the Puppy. This is my favorite story.

I get mommy to read me another story and ask if I can stay up late. Mommy says, "No Candace, time for bed." But mom it's still early and I am not sleepy. You have to let me stay up I wail. Mommy sighs and then she smiles. She kisses me good night and turns out the light.

It's dark and I can't see. But then mommy whispers in my ear, "You're not the boss of me!"

The End.

Printed in the United States
By Bookmasters